DINO-FOOTBALL

LISA WHEELER

ILLUSTRATIONS BY
BARRY GOTT

CAROLRHODA BOOKS MINNEAPOLIS

To the 1974-1980 Pittsburgh Steelers.
Thanks for the wonderful childhood
memories! —L.W.

For Rose, Finn, and Nandi
—B.G.

Text copyright © 2012 by Lisa Wheeler
Illustrations copyright © 2012 by Barry Gott

Carolrhoda Books
A division of Lerner Publishing Group, Inc.
241 First Avenue North
Minneapolis, MN 55401 U.S.A.

Website address: www.lernerbooks.com

Library of Congress Cataloging-in-Publication Data

Wheeler, Lisa, 1963-
    Dino-football / by Lisa Wheeler ; illustrated by Barry Gott.
       p.   cm.
    Summary: Plant-eating dinosaurs face meat-eating dinosaurs in
a football game at the Lava Dome on Mega Bowl Sunday.
    ISBN 978-0-7613-6394-1 (lib. bdg. : alk. paper)
    [1. Stories in rhyme. 2. Football—Fiction. 3. Dinosaurs—Fiction.]
I. Gott, Barry, ill. II. Title.
PZ8.3.W5668Dh 2012
[E]—dc23   2011044346

Manufactured in the United States of America
1 - DP - 7/15/12

Mega Bowl Sunday is finally here!
Excitement's in the atmosphere
for Dino-Football! Stand and cheer!

Inside fans are eager—waiting.
Outside fans? What else—tailgating!

Neither team will play at home.
This game is at the Lava Dome.

The **Greenblade Snackers** look so proud.
The **Redscales** wave up to the crowd.

Pads and helmets for each team.
Uniforms in **red** and **green**.

SNACKERS OFFENSE
Triceratops --QUARTERBACK
Shamosaurus --CENTER
Apatosaurus --LEFT GUARD
Iguanodon --RIGHT GUARD
Plateosaurus --LEFT TACKLE
Stegosaurus --RIGHT TACKLE
Amargasaurus --TIGHT END
Ankylosaurus --WIDE RECEIVER
Mussaurus --WIDE RECEIVER
Pachycephalosaurus --HALFBACK
Gryposaurus --FULLBACK

SNACKERS DEFENSE
Brachiosaurus --NOSE TACKLE
Ultrasaurus --LEFT TACKLE
Diplodocus --RIGHT TACKLE
Pentaceratops --LEFT END
Torosaurus --RIGHT END
Andesaurus --LINEBACKER
Minmi --LINEBACKER
Vulcanodon --LINEBACKER
Maiasaura --CORNERBACK
Hadrosaurus --CORNERBACK
Kentrosaurus--FREE SAFETY

SPECIAL TEAMS
Lesothosaurus --KICKER

REDSCALES OFFENSE
T. rex --QUARTERBACK
Saltopus --CENTER
Gallimimus --LEFT GUARD
Tarbosaurus --RIGHT GUARD
Megalosaurus --LEFT TACKLE
Suchomimus --RIGHT TACKLE
Raptor --TIGHT END
Pterodactyl Twins --WIDE RECEIVERS
Deinonychus --HALFBACK
Troodon --FULLBACK

REDSCALES DEFENSE
Spinosaurus --NOSE TACKLE
Giganotosaurus --LEFT TACKLE
Utahraptor --RIGHT TACKLE
Carnotaurus--LEFT END
Baryonyx --RIGHT END
Allosaurus --LEFT LINEBACKER
Avimimus --RIGHT LINEBACK
Albertosaurus --MIDDLE LINEBACKER
Ingenia --CORNERBACK
Alioramus --CORNERBACK
Dilophosaurus --FREE SAFETY

SPECIAL TEAMS
Compsognathus --KICKER

The coin is tossed. The Redscales win.
Snackers send their kicker in.

To pin the Snackers in their end,
Leso kicks it to the ten.

But **Troodon** is cool and steady,
runs the ball up to the twenty.

Both teams line up eye to eye,
heads down low—tails to the sky.

T. rex is the quarterback.
He calls the play. The ball is snapped.

The **Redscale** linemen make a pocket.
T. rex fires like a rocket.

Raptor does athletic tricks.
A perfect catch. Touchdown! That's six!

Then **Compy** kicks the way he should,
straight through the posts.

"The extra point is good!"

Tricera hands off nice and smooth.
Then tailback, Pachy, makes her move.

With fancy feet, she gets first down
before she's tackled to the ground.

The Snackers run each play the same.
They gain yards with their rushing game.

Field goal range. They go for three.

"The kick is good!"
The refs agree.
It's **Redscales** 7–
Snackers 3.

The **Pterodactyls** watch **T. rex.**
They know their chance is coming next.

He throws it in one twin's direction.
Look out, **Ptero!** Interception!

Kentro gets the takeaway!
This **Snacker** rookie saved the day.

Before the **Redscales** comprehend,
he's Dino-Shuffling in their end.

Leso's kick is true and straight.
The **Snacker** backers celebrate!

Two quarters down and two to go,
here comes the Dino Halftime Show.

A raucous rock band wows the crowd—
electric music blaring loud.

As fans wave flags of green and red,
Good Era blimp floats overhead.

Third quarter starts. 7 to 10.
There's still a long way to the end.

T. rex throws the ball so high.
Ptero catches on the fly.

He hugs the ball, heads down the field.
But there's a Snacker on his heels!

Maia tackles. Down they tumble.

Where'd the ball go? . . . Uh-oh! Fumble!

That ball is loose! That ball is live!
'Til **Suchomimus** takes a dive.

The fans know by his fool expression—
Yes! The **Redscales** keep possession!

Next, **Raptor** for the **Scales** goes long.

He doesn't want to get it wrong.

He sees the ball sail toward his grip.

No time to stall. No time to trip.

Poor **Raptor's** tackled to the ground.
Did he catch the ball?

"Whoo-hoo! Touchdown!"

STOP!

"There's a flag on the play."
What will the officials say?

The football fans must sit and wait
and watch the referees debate.

"Holding. On the defense.
Penalty declined."

The touchdown's good! The **Scales** get six!

The teams line up for **Compy's** kick.

But it's a fake! They go for two.

The **Scales** get stuffed. The **Red** fans BOO!

Snackers—10. Redscales—13.

The crowd is shouting "Let's Go Green!"

Tricera tries a tricky play.

A flea-flicker might save the day.

He lobs the ball to the running back.

Grypo catches—throws it back!

Excited viewers are amused.
But **Utahraptor's** not confused.

This focused tackle's on the attack.
He sacks the **Snacker** quarterback.

Fourth down. No yards. Their option's lame.
Green kicks for **3** and ties the game.

Fourth quarter: T. rex calls the play.
His linemen look the other way.

The quarterback is poised for action—
Doesn't see the team's distraction!

Brach is breathing down his back.

No protection! It's a sack!

Loss of yardage. Linemen pout.

Redscale coaches chew them out.

Redscales flop. It's **Snacker** time!

Clock is ticking. Get in line!

Nose to nose and snout to snout,
Triceratops demands "Time out!"

Green huddles up. The play is called.

Clap! Then break. No time to stall.

The snap is good. The play, perfection.

The ball goes in the right direction.

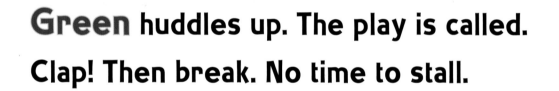

Young **Mussaurus** reaches high.

Plucks the ball out of the sky.

Gets the touchdown! Next, the goal . . .

The Snackers win the Mega Bowl!

Confetti falls! The fans invade!
The coach gets doused with Dino-Ade!

They earned their rings and trophy too.
The Snackers made their dream come true.

It's over now. Fans shed a tear.
What will they watch until next year?

Buy your tickets. Don't be late.
Dino-Wrestling tonight at eight!